THE ROTTEN BOOK

HARPER & ROW, PUBLISHERS
New York, Evanston, and London

THE
ROTTEN
BOOK

by MARY RODGERS

Pictures by Steven Kellogg

THE ROTTEN BOOK
Text copyright © 1969 by Mary Rodgers.
Pictures copyright © 1969 by Steven Kellogg.

Library of Congress Catalog Card Number: 75-85029

For Matthew

"Rotten," said Simon's father.

"Yes, absolutely rotten," said Simon's mother.

"What's rotten?" said Simon. "Is my egg rotten?"

"No, it's not," said Simon's mother, "so stop mucking it around on your plate."

"*I'm* eating my egg *all* up," said Simon's sister.

"Yup, rotten through and through," said Simon's father.

"Well, if it's not my egg, what *is*?" said Simon.

"What is what?"

"What is rotten?"

"A little boy you don't even know, dear," said Simon's mother.

"What beats me is that kid's got everything," said his father. "A million toys, parents who love him—Simon, what about your egg—an adorable younger sister...A kid like that is headed for real trouble—your egg, Simon, your egg—and if *I* were that kid's father..."

"But what did he do, Dad?" asked Simon. "What did he *do* that was so rotten?"

"Never you mind, darling," said his mother.

"That kid's going to land up in jail one of these days—egg, EGG, *EAT THAT EGG*—and it'll be nobody's fault but his own," said Simon's father, who went on talking and talking and talking to Simon's mother while Simon sat there thinking and thinking and thinking.

I wonder what he did, Simon thought. If he hates eggs, would he put them in his napkin and put the napkin behind the radiator? And wipe his eggy mouth on his shirt?

Maybe he'd be rotten in school. Like letting the guinea pig loose. And pouring his juice into the turtles. And fighting.

"Children, children, we don't grab. We take turns. And when Ashley is finished with the truck, then *you* may have it," the teacher would say.

So then maybe he'd bite Ashley! And Ashley would have to go to the nurse. Maybe he might even bite a GIRL called Ashley.

When he came home for lunch maybe his mother would say,
"Here, darling, let me tie your shoes before you trip."
And he'd say, "I *like* them that way."
And she'd say, "Your hot dog is waiting for you."
And he'd say, "I don't want nothing for lunch."
And she'd say, "*Any*thing, not nothing."
And he'd say, "No, I don't," and waste a whole hot dog.

Maybe he'd go to his room for a nap and be destructive. There'd be a lot of destructive things he could do in his own room. Pulling down window shades. Peeling off the wallpaper. Throwing stuff out the window. Looking for a tiny hole in his sheet and making the tiny hole bigger.

Or maybe he'd come out of his room before his nap was up and do a lot of *noisy* destructive things—like getting out the vacuum cleaner and sucking up the plants on the window sill and all the buttons in the sewing box. Buttons could probably wreck a vacuum cleaner faster than anything except marbles. Maybe he'd use marbles.

Maybe he'd do rotten things in the supermarket. If he made a tower of baby-food jars and it fell down, there would be a big mush of Apple Gel and Beef-Liver-with-Beef-Heart and all that gunk. The manager would get sore. "Hey, this kid's a public menace! Call the cops and get him out of here."

Or maybe he would just zing one of those carts up and down the aisles yelling, "Here comes Batman, get out of the way," which everyone would do except for an old lady who wouldn't move fast enough, so he'd knock her down and run over her and almost cut her in two, and he wouldn't even say, "Sorry."

Maybe if he got home, he'd put Silly Putty in his sister's hair. Silly Putty wouldn't come out of hair too well, so then he'd probably say, "Let's play Barber."

She'd say, "What's that?"

He'd say, "That's when you sit down and stay very still and I take these big scissors and get rid of this mess here in the back."

Then she'd say, "How does it look now?"

And he'd say, "Oh, much better. Except now the front isn't the same as the back, so sit very still and I'll fix the front."

"You're getting it in my eyes," she'd say.

"Well, close your mouth and close your eyes, and soon you'll see a nice surprise," he'd say, cutting the front part to match the back part.

"*Now* how do you like yourself?"

"I don't. I hate it. I look just like you, and I hate *you*!" she'd scream.

"Oh, shut up. You know Mom hates noise," he'd say and shove her in a closet and lock the door and hide the key. And then he'd turn on the hi-fi and the TV and FM and sing "Row, Row, Row Your Boat" as loudly as he could, so nobody could hear his sister screaming and banging and kicking in the closet.

His mother would say, "Where's your little sister? I haven't seen her around lately."

He'd say, "Gee, Mom, search me."

She'd say, "Don't be silly. I'm not going to search you. I can see she's not on you. I'm going to call your father at the office and the police and fire department."

First the fire department would come. They'd look in the chimney and the oven and the toy chest and the refrigerator.

Then the police would come. They'd dust for fingerprints and pick up bits of evidence, like scissors and a wad of Silly Putty with long blond hair on it, which they'd put in an envelope for the files.

Then his father would come and say, "It's so noisy in here I can't hear myself think. Turn off the hi-fi and the TV and the FM."

"I hear a kid screaming," a policeman would say.

"Yeah, I think the kid's in this closet," a fireman would say.

"Where's the key to the closet, son?" his father would say.
"Search me," he'd say again, and they would. They'd search
him all over and turn him upside down, and the key would
fall out of his pocket, and they'd unlock the door.

"Hey, lady, you got a little boy in here, not a little girl. Do you want us to keep looking for your little girl?" the fireman and the policeman would say.

"This *is* my little girl!" the mother would howl. "Only where's all her hair?"

"Some of it's in here," the policeman would say, holding up the envelope. "I'm afraid, madam, that your little boy is under arrest."

"That's fine by me," his mother would say.

"Whoopee!" his sister would say.

"Fair enough," his father would say.

"Jail's too good for a rotten kid like that," the fireman would say, and they'd all stand around in the doorway and watch the policeman drive off in the squad car with the boy sitting beside him in handcuffs.

He'd probably spend the rest of his life in jail with nothing to eat but bread and water. Probably he'd never even get an egg for breakfast....

"Boy, this is a good egg," said Simon.
"That's nice, dear," said his mother.
"This sure is the best egg I ever ate, Mom," said Simon.

"I'm glad you like it, dear," said his mother. "Would you like another one?"

"Oh, no. No, thank you very much," said Simon quickly.

"I'll just finish my milk here and wipe my mouth nicely on this napkin and take my plate out to the kitchen."

"That's very helpful of you, Simon," said his father.

"Happy to do it, Dad," said Simon, and he took his mother's plate and his father's plate and even his sister's plate out to the kitchen.

"Now I'm going to make my bed and clean up my room and brush my teeth and get all dressed and ready for school so I won't be late," said Simon.

"What on earth got into *him* today?" said Simon's mother.

"Search me," said Simon's father.